The Yellow ÁO DÀI

written by **Hanh Bui**

illustrated by **Minnie Phan**

Feiwel and Friends

New York

Áo dài is pronounced *ow-yai* (rhyming with "now fly").

A Feiwel and Friends Book
An imprint of Macmillan Publishing Group, LLC
120 Broadway, New York, NY 10271 • mackids.com

Our books may be purchased in bulk for promotional, educational, or business use.
Please contact your local bookseller or the Macmillan Corporate and Premium Sales Department at
(800) 221-7945 ext. 5442 or by email at MacmillanSpecialMarkets@macmillan.com.

Library of Congress Cataloging-in-Publication Data is available.

First edition, 2023
Book design by Melisa Vuong
This book was illustrated in Procreate and Photoshop.
Feiwel and Friends logo designed by Filomena Tuosto
Printed in China by RR Donnelley Asia Printing Solutions Ltd., Dongguan City, Guangdong Province

ISBN 978-1-250-84206-0 (hardcover)
1 3 5 7 9 10 8 6 4 2

For Tony, Justin, Nathan and Lauren: Your love makes all things possible —H.B.

For Loan: Thank you for believing in me —M.P.

It was the day before International Day at school, and Naliah couldn't help but be a little nervous.

She loved to sing and dance. Last year, Naliah had taught her classmates a Vietnamese song. This year, she was performing her favorite traditional Vietnamese dance, and she wanted to do her best.

Naliah had learned the Fan Dance from her mother, who had learned it from *her* mother. In Vietnam, Naliah's grandmother had led the Fan Dance at the Mid-Autumn Festival, which celebrates the end of the harvest season.

Naliah knew exactly what to wear: her special áo dài. She had been waiting until now to practice in her fanciest dress so it wouldn't be wrinkled for her performance.

But when she tried it on, Naliah was dismayed to find it was too snug. She must have grown since she last wore it!

Maybe Mom has one that I could use, she thought.

Naliah tiptoed into her mom's room, where colorful áo dàis cascaded from the closet like a hanging garden of flowers. She spotted a yellow one embroidered with swans and water lilies.

Yellow: the color of happiness and forsythia blossoms.

Naliah slipped it on.

The dress pooled around her like water.

She rolled up the sleeves, tugged it up around her waist, and cinched it with a belt.

Then she unfolded Mom's wooden fans and began to practice.

Naliah reached up on her tippy toes. She twirled and swayed, like petals blowing in the breeze.

She imagined herself as a graceful lotus blossom, gliding across a stage.

As she twirled, the long dress tangled around her feet, and . . .

Rrrrippp!

"Oh no!" Naliah squeaked. *Will Mom be mad?*

She heard her mother's footsteps coming down the hall. Naliah hid the áo dài in the back of the closet, burying it as deep as she could.

"Naliah?" Mom asked. "What are you doing, little one?"

Naliah glanced away, her heart racing. "I'm looking for an áo dài to wear for International Day tomorrow. Mine is too small."

Mom smiled and said, "I thought you might need a new one."

She handed Naliah a present. Tucked between layers of lavender tissue paper was a beautiful áo dài the color of happiness and forsythia blossoms. Butterflies covered the front of the dress in all the shades of the rainbow.

"Thank you, Mom. I love it!" Naliah cried. "It's the perfect áo dài for the Fan Dance!"

"I'm so glad you like it," Mom said. "I have a special yellow áo dài, too."

Naliah's stomach churned. "But . . . blue is your favorite color."

"Yes, but yellow was your grandmother's favorite color.
She brought the áo dài with her when she left Vietnam."

Sadness rose in Naliah's chest.

Then Mom took a photo out of her keepsake box. Naliah peered closer.

Are those water lilies? And swans? Oh no . . .

"Your grandmother wore it when she performed the Fan Dance in her village," Mom explained. "She was chosen to be the Mid-Autumn Festival Princess because she was the most graceful dancer of all."

Mom looked around the closet. "Hmm, I wonder where I put it . . ."

Tears welled in Naliah's eyes. She took a breath and slowly dug out the yellow áo dài. "Is this it?"

"Yes, that's the one!" But Mom's smile faded when she saw the hole in the fabric.

Naliah looked down at her feet. "I'm so sorry," she whispered. "I tried on your áo dài to practice the Fan Dance. But I fell, and it ripped! I ruined Grandmother's special dress."

Mom was silent.

Naliah held her breath.

Mom knelt and gathered Naliah in her arms. "I know you didn't mean to rip it. When I was a little girl, I also loved trying on my mother's áo dàis. I tore the very same dress."

"You did?!" Naliah gasped.

"Do you see this lily pad?" Mom asked. "Your grandmother embroidered it over the hole that I made. We can sew another one over the new hole."

Hope bloomed in Naliah's heart. "Can you sew a frog instead? You always say frogs are lucky."

Mom opened her sewing box. Naliah threaded the needle with a shade of green that reminded her of moss-covered rocks. When Mom finished, a cute little frog sat on top of a lovely lily blossom.

Naliah hugged and sniff kissed her mom. "You fixed it!"

"Your grandmother's áo dài is even more special now that it has your lucky frog on it," Mom said, planting sweet sniff kisses on Naliah's head. "And when you grow up, this áo dài will be yours."

The next morning, before the International Day celebration, Naliah slipped on her new áo dài. It fit just right.

Mom wore her yellow áo dài, too.

"Mom, you look like a Mid-Autumn Princess, just like Grandmother in the photo!" Naliah said.

Mom beamed. "Thank you, sweetheart. *You* are a Mid-Autumn Princess, too."

Even though Naliah had practiced, she felt like the butterflies on her dress were fluttering in her stomach. All her classmates and teachers would be watching her.

"Will I be as graceful as Grandmother?" Naliah asked quietly.

"As graceful as a lotus in full bloom," Mom whispered in her ear. "Your grandmother would be so proud of you."

Naliah's fans whirled as she floated across the stage. The butterflies no longer fluttered in her stomach.

Instead, they flitted and
flapped where they belonged:
on her yellow áo dài.

And just for a moment, Naliah imagined herself dancing the Fan Dance with her mother and grandmother in the meadows of Vietnam. She could almost smell the scent of jasmine blossoms.

She truly felt like a Mid-Autumn Princess.

A Note from the Author

This story is inspired by my daughter and her beloved grandmother (my mother-in-law). My daughter was very young when her grandmother passed away. My mother-in-law's beautiful áo dàis are treasured family heirlooms that allow all of us to stay connected to her through memories and the stories she shared with us. My mother-in-law was crowned Mid-Autumn Princess when she was a schoolgirl. When my daughter wears her yellow áo dài, she, too, feels like a Mid-Autumn Princess.

As a young girl learning English, I also performed the Fan Dance for my school's International Day. I loved celebrating my Vietnamese heritage with my teachers and classmates. It was the one day when other children tasted Vietnamese food, admired traditional dances, and learned the Vietnamese language. Now my daughter and I participate in her school's International Day together. It is my hope that my children and all children recognize that their family stories matter and see themselves between the pages of the books they read.

In Loving Memory of Yvonne Đinh Thuỳ Mai.

A Note from the Illustrator

Reading the story of Naliah reminded me of the special connection my mother and I have to mending and handsewing clothing. Growing up in America, I experienced what many children of immigrants do: losing one's mother tongue as English becomes the predominate language spoken. Without common fluency, my mother and I discovered ways to connect creatively. Where we lacked words, we had art. My childhood was spent learning how to sew, knit, and make other crafts with my mom. Her love did not always need to be spoken; I knew from the way she guided my hands and sat by my side that I was special. Just like Naliah and her mother, the skills taught to me were passed on from one generation to another. Every needle threaded was a connection to my ancestors. Thank you Hanh, for your beautiful story!

Minnie, her mom, and two sisters wearing beautiful áo dài in many colors

Glossary

áo dài: A traditional Vietnamese dress worn by all genders but most commonly by girls and women. It is a long tunic dress with slits on either side. Áo dàis are blank canvases for beautiful art painted on or embroidered by hand. Swans, peacocks, cranes, flowers, butterflies, and natural landscapes are just a few examples of common images on áo dàis.

Fan Dance: A popular dance performed at schools and festivals for special occasions. It was also a traditional dance featured in royal palaces in ancient times. The dancers sway like flowers in the breeze.

Mid-Autumn Festival: Also known as "Tet Trung Thu," this is a popular holiday in Vietnam. It is celebrated in late September or early October, depending on the lunar calendar. The Mid-Autumn Festival marks the end of the harvest season and the beginning of more family time after the busy days in September harvesting crops. Children parade from house to house carrying paper lanterns shaped like fish, butterflies, flowers, and stars, playing and singing in the moonlight while eating mooncakes.

Mid-Autumn Princess: Many schools and towns in Vietnam host annual Mid-Autumn Festivals. Girls dress up in beautiful áo dàis to perform popular Vietnamese dances as part of the festivities. It is considered an honor to be chosen as the Mid-Autumn Princess, who represents her school or town during the celebrations.

sniff kiss: Sniff kissing is how Vietnamese parents and grandparents show affection for children or grandchildren. With their noses, elders breathe in the sweetness of their children by sniff kissing them on their cheeks, their foreheads, or the tops of their heads. Children also like to give sniff kisses.